HALLOWEEN
A B C

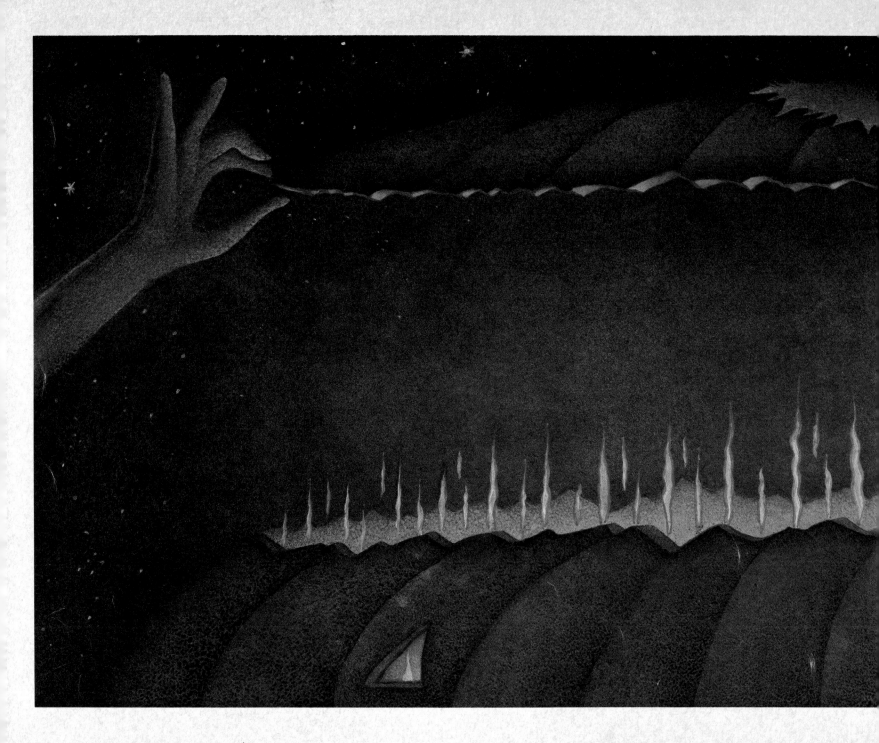

HALLOWEEN ABC

Poems by **Eve Merriam** · Illustrations by **Lane Smith**

Macmillan Publishing Company   New York / Collier Macmillan Publishers   London

Text copyright © 1987 by Eve Merriam
Illustrations copyright © 1987 by Lane Smith
All rights reserved. No part of this book may be reproduced or transmitted
in any form or by any means, electronic or mechanical, including
photocopying, recording, or by any information storage and retrieval
system, without permission in writing from the Publisher.
Macmillan Publishing Company, 866 Third Avenue, New York, NY 10022
Collier Macmillan Canada, Inc.
Printed in the United States of America

First American Edition   10 9 8 7 6 5 4 3

The text of this book is set in 14 point Goudy Old Style.
The illustrations are rendered in oil on board.

Library of Congress Cataloging-in-Publication Data
Merriam, Eve, date.
Halloween A B C.
Summary: Each letter of the alphabet introduces a
different, spooky aspect of Halloween.
I. Halloween – Juvenile poetry. 2. Alphabet rhymes.
[1. Halloween – Poetry. 2. Alphabet] I. Smith, Lane,
ill. II. Title. III. Title: Halloween ABC.
PS3525.E639H34 1987 811'.54 [E] 86-23772
ISBN 0-02-766870-3

For Marian Reiner
—E.M.

For Mom and Dad
—L.S.

Apple

Apple,
sweet apple,
what do you hide?
Wormy and
squirmy,
rotten inside.

Apple,
sweet apple,
so shiny and red,
taste it,
don't waste it,
come and be fed.

Delicious,
malicious;
one bite and
you're dead.

Bat

Bats in the belfry
lurk on high.
When midnight chimes,
shadows fly.

Umbrella wings,
beware, beware.
A silent swoop,
a cobwebby scare,
a rush in the darkness,
a brush against your hair.

Shiver and tremble
and don't dare shriek;
the creatures can tell
if you're faint or weak.

By dawn they're back
in their dim dank lair
up in the rafters:
waiting, waiting there.

Crawler

Creepy crawlers
creepy crawlers
creepy crawlers clutchers

terrible feelers
horrible touchers

creeping in your hair
crawling on your skin
nobody knows
how they get in

creeping from the north
crawling from the south
creeping down your forehead
crawling in your mouth

creeping on your tongue
crawling down your throat
into your gizzard
where they float float float.

Demon

Diabolic demons
dance in the dell,
diabolic demons
cast their spell:

"Make this spot
infernally hot,
put your hate in,
Satan;
pass the pitchfork, please,
Mephistopheles;
Lucifer,
Beelzebub,
come when we call.
The devil,
the devil,
the devil
with it all!"

Elf

Little, littler, littlest sprite
laughs in secret, hides from sight;
can curdle milk, can tangle silk,
can guard from harm, can bring a charm.
Kind or wicked, true elves find
it all depends on humankind.

Fiend

A fiend with fiendish glee
is happy as can be,
mixing fiendish drinks,
stinking up the sinks,
unwinding all the clocks,
mismatching all the socks,
growing grass upon its head,
and never ever going to bed.

Ghost

More gruesome than any groan,
more dreadful than any moan,
most trembling, terrifying sight:
white silence in the dark of night.

House

Why do the curtains blow?
What do the floorboards know?
What is that splotch on the wall?
What is that clank in the hall?
Why does a sudden light appear,
and why does it suddenly disappear?

Icicle

An icy stabbing so swiftly done,
the victim scarcely felt it.
The police are baffled:
"Where's the weapon?"
The sun shines down to melt it.

Jack-o'lantern

Jack-o'-lantern,
jack-o'-lantern,
all aglow,
jack-o'-lantern,
jack-o'-lantern,
don't you know

your head is hollow,
you're missing teeth,
you've got no brains
and nothing underneath.

Jack-o'-lantern,
jack-o'-lantern,
squish squash squush,
when Halloween's over
you'll turn to mush.

Jack-o'-lantern,
jack-o'-lantern,
crybaby cry,
you'll end up
in pumpkin pie.

Key

"Follow me"
spells the key
that opens a gate
that leads to a wood
where a tower stands tall,
and the door of the tower
leads to a stair
that winds all the way
to the topmost floor
where a narrow hall
leads to a room
with a trunk inside,
and the lid of the trunk
springs open wide
to show a key
that spells "Follow me."

Lair

Lunging, plunging through the woods,
past the torchlight, past the fire,
loping, leaping, leading on
through the brambles, through the brier,
luring you into its lair.
Close your heart to what is there,
close your heart to what you learn,
or you may be taken in
and you may not return.

Mask

Guises, disguises,
all kinds of surprises:
A peasant's a king,
a king's a knave,
a knave's a donkey,
a donkey's a slave.
Conceal, conceal,
peel off and reveal
the mask that no one detects:
your face that the mirror reflects.

Nightmare

Nay nay nay
never get away
writhing writhing
in woe woe woe
too late to tell
friend from foe
closing in
for the kill
try to escape
chances are nil
nail you down
box you in a crate
stamp you null and void
seal your fate.

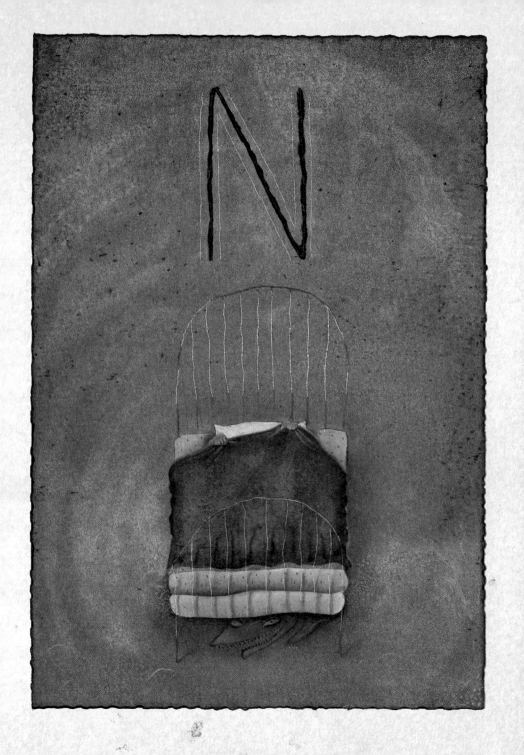

Owl

Who
who
who did it
who?

Who spilled the beans
who broke the news
who stepped into
somebody's shoes?

Who
who
who did it
who?

Who slipped the word
who hit a snag
who let the cat
out of the bag?

Who did the deed
who gets the blame
who is the culprit
What is your name?

Pet

A pet to pat, a pal of a pet,
a pet the family won't forget,
a pet that pants and drools and yaps
and leaves a little spot in laps,
a pet that's not the least bit vicious,
yet finds the neighbors quite nutritious.

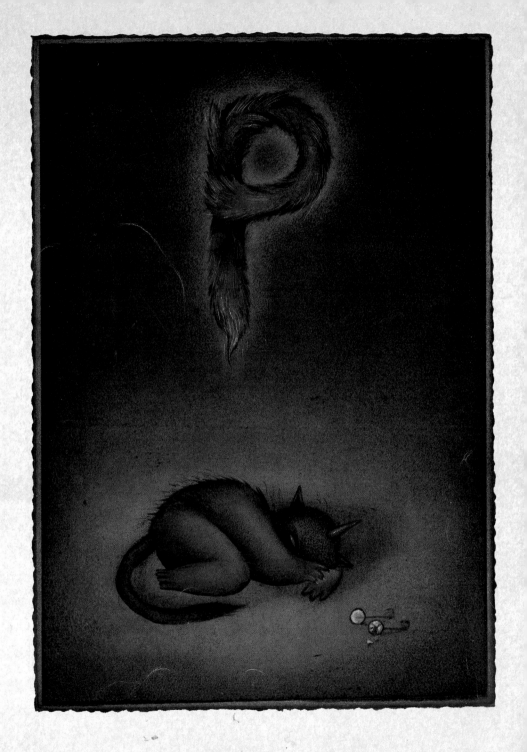

Question

Write it on the North Wind,
bury it in a wooden cask;
what is the question
that you dare not ask?

Rope

Twist the hemp
spin the flax
don't fall into
the pavement cracks.

Bind fasten
entwine braid
step from the sunlight
into the shade.

Hoist the rope
keep it loose
hoist the rope
for what use:

to lift a sunken cargo?
or be a hangman's noose?

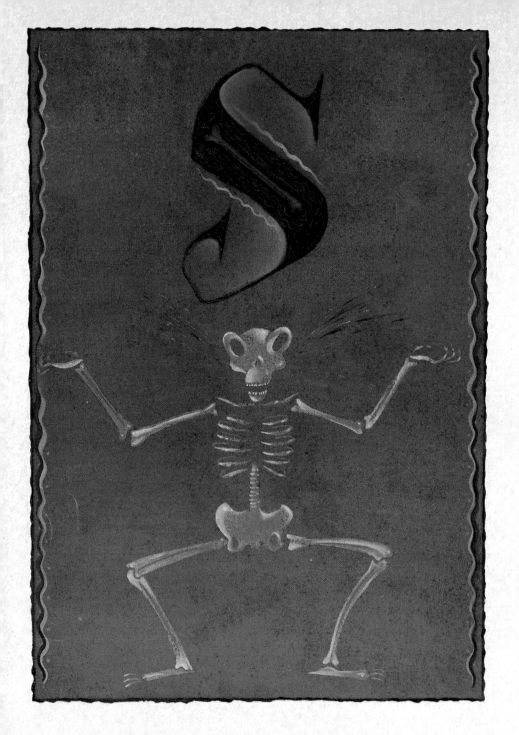

Skeleton

Clack clack clack
up the stair;
run to look—
no one's there.

Clack clack clack
at the window panes:
merry pranksters
or *grave remains?*

Trap

Get a trap set a trap
trap trap trap
tap you slap you
try to wriggle free
coax you hoax you
snare take care
catch you latch you
never get free
hook you crook you
can't catch me.

Umbrella

Umbrella, umbrella,
duck under, duck under;
the sky is a rage of
lightning and thunder!

More and more downpour,
deluging drenching,
abhorrent torrent,
no stopping sopping.

It's raining pitchforks,
it's raining cats and dogs
and loathsome toadsome
bulging bullfrogs.

Viper

Viper, viper,
spiteful sniper,
snake in the grass, lowdown, base,
smiling, smiling to your face,
virulent villain, venomous, vile,
darting poison with a snaky smile.

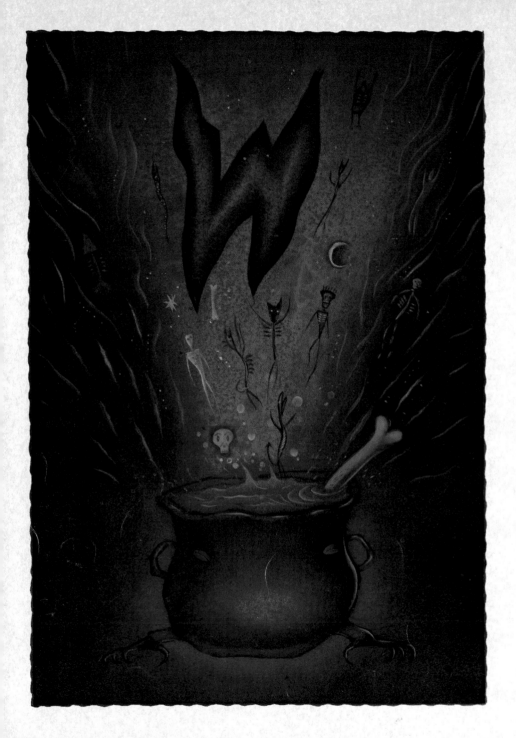

Witchery

Which, which,
which witchery?
Nectar of nightshade
or venom of bee?

Which, which,
which woeful bane?
Juice of the hemlock
or brimstone with rain?

Which, which,
which plaguey pox?
Soup bowls of toadstools
or mouse broth in crocks?

Which, which,
which should we choose?
Buckets of slimy
or barrels of ooze?

Which wicked wickedness,
which will we serve?
Well, which pretty poison
do *you* deserve?

Xylophone

Xylophone tones
xylophone bones

bones to clang
bones to bang

bones to bing
bones to bong:

Are they the bones
of old King Kong?

Yeast

Stir it in the brew
stir it in the bread
rise rise
seethe spread
fuss fume
foam spume
spread and spread
and spread and spread
and spread and spread and spread.

Zero

Round blank
Round blank
Only bubbles
mark where it sank.

What was the secret,
what was the prize?
Nothing but hollow
holes for eyes.

Where did it come from,
and where did it go?
No one alive
will ever know.

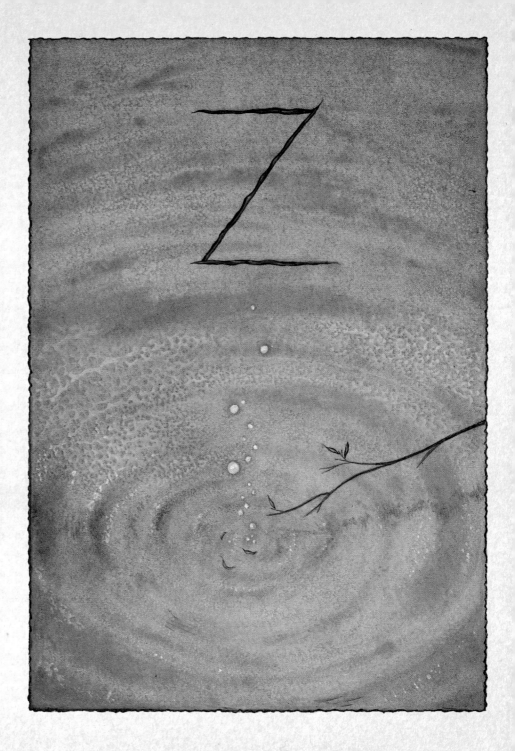